Bruce The Little Blue Spruce

A
Silverline™
B O O K S
PRODUCTION
A DIVISION OF
Shadowline™ / image®

Silverline™
B O O K S

A DIVISION OF

Shadowline™ / image®

www.shadowlinecomics.com/silverline
www.kris-korner.com

BRUCE THE LITTLE BLUE SPRUCE (December 2008) is published by Image Comics, Inc. 1942 University Ave, Suite 305, Berkeley, CA 94704. Image and its logos are ® and © 2008 Image Comics, Inc. Shadowline and it's logos are ™ and © by Shadowline, LLC. BRUCE THE LITTLE BLUE SPRUCE and its logos are ™ and © Kristen K. Simon 2008. All rights reserved. The characters, events and stories in this publication are entirely fictional. No portion of this book may be reproduced, save for purposes of review, without the expressed written consent of Ms. Simon. PRINTED IN HONG KONG.

Written by
Kristen Koerner Simon

Illustrated by
Jim Valentino
Book Design, Publisher

Colored by
Avery Butterworth

Lettered by
Jason Hanley

Dedications

"To my family, who saw this book from the very beginning, and to my nephew Dane Scott Koerner, who reminds us daily what it's like to be a kid.

And special thanks to Jim Valentino for capturing everything perfectly and for bringing this little story of mine to life."

-Kristen Koerner Simon

"To my sons Aaron and Joel, who gave my life meaning and my heart wings.

And to Kris, may all your dreams be fulfilled."

-Jim Valentino

There once was a
little tree that was
planted in a very
large forest.

The little tree always
knew that he was different,
but he was too young to
understand why.

He didn't even know
what those differences
were.

On the day he was planted, the new little tree was visited by the local welcome wagon, a small group of cheerful field mice who weren't very bright.

There was **Smudge**, who loved desserts! **Bailey**, who was a bit loopy in the head. **Butterscotch** was the girl in the group, and **Ming** was the one who made all the decisions.

At this announcement, all of the mice looked closer at the little tree, and they noticed that sure enough, he was more of a light blue than green!

And every mouse knew that Christmas trees were green!

Bruce was sad.

He had always assumed that he was planted in the forest because, like all the other trees, he was to grow big and tall, just for Christmas, and then bring joy to a special family during that Holy season.

He didn't know how he knew this. He just did.

He wondered why he had been put in the forest, if not to be a Christmas tree.

At this, the mice all squeaked in horror and ran away. The little tree swayed, upset at what the mice had said.

It was true; there were no other Bruce trees in the forest.

How was he to make a special family happy if no one wanted him?

No, I don't think so. I'm blue the whole year round.

I wanted to be a Christmas tree for a special family to make them *happy.*

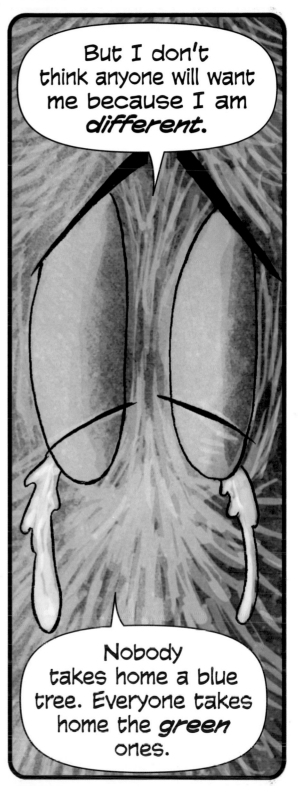

But I don't think anyone will want me because I am *different.*

Nobody takes home a blue tree. Everyone takes home the *green* ones.

The years passed by, and with each year passing, the little tree grew bigger and bigger, until finally he was just the right size to fit into a special family's home to make them happy.

He hoped against hope that he would be picked, as the families wandered through the area in search of their perfect tree.

The little mice had come back often to taunt and tease Bruce, but Jack was always there to lift his spirits and chase away the mice when he was around.

The end of the year was getting closer and closer. Bruce knew that if he wasn't picked this year, he would be too big next year. Over and over he heard parents saying to their children,

How about this *blue* one?

Bruce's spirits would soar, only to come plummeting down when the children replied,

We want a *green* one!

At last there were only a few trees left, and the families were becoming less and less frequent.

Bruce had just about given up hope when a family came around the bend.

Bruce puffed up proudly, determined to look regal and majestic, despite his odd coloring.

The mother looked closely at Bruce and smiled widely. The children cheered and hugged each their parents.

Bruce beamed
with pride. Jack
was right.

It took a special family to
notice a special tree, and
Bruce had no doubts that
he was indeed, a very
special tree.

He would make this
family's Christmas
the happiest one
ever.

THE END.

About the Author

Kristen Koerner Simon was born and raised in Chicago and still lives there. She has an African Fat-tailed Gecko named Chilly, and adores her Tivo. She has Jason Simon to thank for her easy-to-pronounce last name, and is also very close to her family, the Koerner's. Currently, Kristen edits comic books for Shadowline, a partner studio of Image Comics. She loves her job, and hopes to continue doing it for a long, long time.

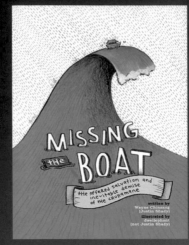